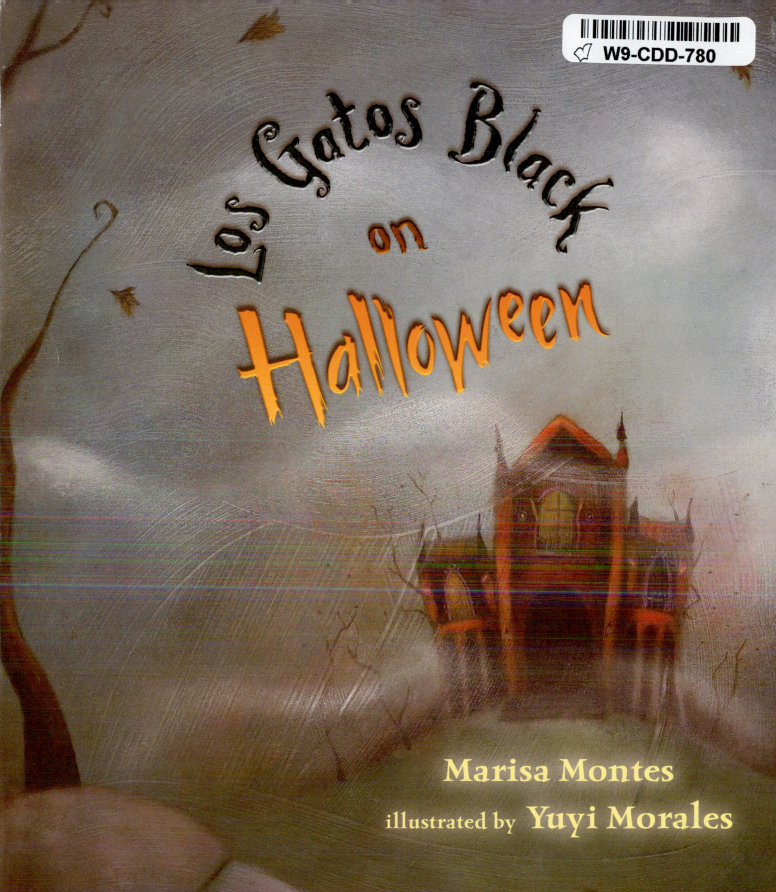

Los Gatos Black on Halloween

Marisa Montes

illustrated by **Yuyi Morales**

SQUARE
FISH

HENRY HOLT AND COMPANY ◇ NEW YORK

Los *gatos* black with eyes of green,
Cats slink and creep on Halloween.
With *ojos* keen that squint and gleam—
They yowl, they hiss . . . they sometimes scream.

Las calabazas, fat and round,
Carved pumpkins guard a hallowed ground.
Their eerie faces burning bright
Form spooky beacons in the night.

Las brujas guide their broomsticks high,

The witches on *escobas* fly.

Above the earth, before the moon,

They swoop and swish and swoosh, and soon . . .

. . . *Los esqueletos rattle bones.*
The skeletons with creaks and groans
Delight the night, in moonbeams dance—
An awkward bow, a clattering prance.

Next los fantasmas drag their chains;
The ghosts, the phantoms, shriek their pains.
Now come the ghouls. Then zombies march
Beneath the trees where branches arch.

October's *luna*, full and bright,
The fall moon lights a vampire's bite.
La momia walks, the mummy stalks,
And faraway a lone loon mocks.

At medianoche midnight strikes—
The witching hour the werewolf likes.
The bloodhounds bay, *los perros* howl.
Beware! The wolfman's on the prowl.

The gravesites shiver, headstones shake.
Las tumbas open, tombs awake.
The corpses with their cold, dead eyes,
Los muertos from their coffins rise.

And in a slow and strange parade,
The creatures of the night invade
A haunted *casa*, long asleep—
The mansion's secrets buried deep.

Yes, by the magic of this night,
This noche filled with chills and fright,
The monsters crowd the Haunted Hall—
Los monstruos throw a monstrous ball.

The thing that monsters most abhor
Are human *niños* at the door!
Of all the horrors they have seen,
The WORST are kids on Halloween!

GLOSSARY

bruja / las brujas (BROO-hah / lahs BROO-hahs). Witch; the witches.

calabaza / las calabazas (kah-lah-VAH-sah / lahs kah-lah-VAH-sahs). Pumpkin; the pumpkins.

casa (KAH-sah). House.

dedo / dedos (DEH-doh / DEH-dohs). Finger; fingers.

escoba / escobas (es-KOH-vah / es-KOH-vahs). Broom; brooms.

esqueleto / los esqueletos (es-keh-LEH-toh / lohs es-keh-LEH-tohs). Skeleton; the skeletons.

fantasma / los fantasmas (fan-TAHZ-mah / lohs fan-TAHZ-mahs). Phantom; the phantoms.

gato / los gatos (GAH-toh / lohs GAH-tohs). Cat; the cats.

las / los (lahs / lohs). The.

luna (LOO-nah). Moon.

medianoche (meh-deeyah-NOH-cheh). Midnight.

momia / la momia (MOH-meeyah / lah MOH-meeyah). Mummy; the mummy.

monstruo / los monstruos (MOHNS-trwoh / lohs MOHNS-trwohs). Monster; the monsters.

muerto / los muertos (MOOWARE-toh / lohs MOOWARE-tohs). Dead; the dead.

música / la música (MOO-see-kah / lah MOO-see-kah). Music; the music.

niño / niños (NEE-nyoh / NEE-nyohs). Child; children.

noche (NOH-cheh). Night.

ojo / ojos (OH-hoh / OH-hohs). Eye; eyes.

perro / los perros (PEH-rroh / lohs PEH-rrohs). Dog; the dogs.

puerta / la puerta (POOWARE-tah / lah POOWARE-tah). Door; the door.

tres (trehs). Three.

tumba / las tumbas (TOOM-bah / lahs TOOM-bahs). Tomb; the tombs.

For Tití Carmín
because you have always
believed in me
—M. M.

For Tim O'Meara, who taught me
how to love in English:
Yo le adoro con todo mi español
—Y. M.

SQUARE
FISH
An Imprint of Macmillan
175 Fifth Avenue, New York, NY 10010
mackids.com

Square Fish and the Square Fish logo are trademarks of Macmillan and are used by Henry Holt and Company, LLC under license from Macmillan.

Our books may be purchased in bulk for promotional, educational, or business use. Please contact your local bookseller or the Macmillan Corporate and Premium Sales Department at (800) 221-7945 ext. 5442 or by e-mail at MacmillanSpecialMarkets@macmillan.com.

Library of Congress Cataloging-in-Publication Data
Montes, Marisa.
Los gatos black on Halloween / Marisa Montes; illustrated by Yuyi Morales.
p.   cm.
Summary: Easy to read, rhyming text about Halloween night incorporates Spanish words, from las brujas riding their broomsticks to los monstruos whose monstrous ball is interrupted by a true horror.
ISBN 978-1-250-07945-9 (paperback)
[1. Halloween—Fiction. 2. Spanish language—Vocabulary—Fiction. 3. Stories in rhyme.] I. Morales, Yuyi, ill. II. Title.
PZ8.3.M775Gat 2006   [E]—dc22   2005020049

Originally published in the United States by Henry Holt and Company, LLC
First Square Fish Edition: 2016 / Book designed by Laurent Linn
Square Fish logo designed by Filomena Tuosto

3 5 7 9 10 8 6 4 2